# a note from the author

The story of "Will Powers - Where There's a Will There's a Way" is basically my story. I started playing guitar when I was 11 years old, growing up in a small town in Georgia. I was a good kid with amazing parents who made sure I believed that whatever I put my mind to I could accomplish. They instilled in me a strong work ethic. They told me I didn't have to be naturally the best to be on top, but that I had to work harder than everyone else. In 8th grade, I tried out for marching band and didn't make it. It's funny to think about now, but that setback didn't discourage my love of music. At 19, I knew I wanted to play music for a living. I studied music in college and practiced for hours every day for years. My hard work and dedication has paid off, as I get to live my dream every day. In this book, I want to show kids the power of confidence and the importance of a strong work ethic. Personally, I owe everything to my parents who instilled those values in me. Many years, and many shows later, even with three Grammy awards under my belt, I'm still working as hard as ever. I hope you enjoy "Will Powers."

## ~ Coy Bowles

A POST HILL PRESS BOOK

WILL POWERS
Where There's a Will There's a Way
© 2016 by Coy Bowles

ISBN 978-1-68261-134-0
ISBN [eBook] 978-1-68261-135-7

The text was set in Chowderhead
Chowderhead © Font Diner, www.fontdiner.com
Cover design and illustrations by Brian de Tagyos

# Will Powers
## Where There's a Will
## There's a Way

Story by Coy Bowles
Illustrations by Brian de Tagyos

# There once was a boy named Will Powers.

He had a lot of friends
and they would play for hours.

He loved **trains** and **planes**
and **meatballs** and **cars**,

Will was good at everything.
He made good grades.
He had good manners.

He could run,

he could jump,
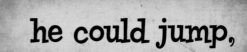

and he could go
bananas!

Will played guitar but he was
a little lazy.
If it didn't come easy, it drove
him crazy.

He had ribbons and trophies
from things he had won.
But practicing guitar was too hard
and no fun.

He came home from school one day
with a super-sad face.
He had tried out for the
school talent show
but didn't even place.

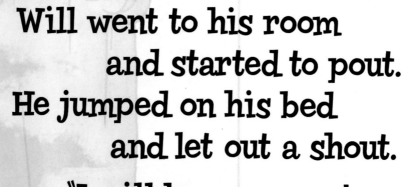

Will went to his room
and started to pout.
He jumped on his bed
and let out a shout.

"I will be awesome!
I will totally rock!
But don't expect me to practice
forever nonstop!"

Will grabbed his guitar and he started to play.
Before he knew it he had practiced all day.

He strummed
and he sang and started to dance.
He said,
"Tomorrow I'll ask for just
one more chance."

He went to his teacher, nervous as could be.
He was sweating and shaking
like a jumpy monkey.

He played his guitar
and she was very impressed.
She said,
"If you keep practicing you
could be the best!"

She said, "Will, you have talent
but practicing isn't easy.
I'll let you into the talent show
but you cannot be lazy."

Will ran home excited
as a puppy with two tails.

He ran straight to his room
and started practicing scales.

The talent show was two weeks away and he had work to do.

He couldn't just lie around
taking naps
like a lion at the zoo.

He practiced and
practiced
for hours and hours.

He practiced at home,
on the bus,
and even in the shower.

The day finally arrived. It was time for the show. Will had been practicing and was ready to go.

Everyone at school
and all his friends were so impressed.
He was glowing with pride.
He had passed the test.

Other kids in the show
had been practicing for years.
Will knew winning was tough,
but he was happy he got cheers.

He placed second in the talent show and loved his new ribbon.
His teacher was proud that he was so driven.

His parents hugged him
and took him to his favorite ice cream shop.
He learned a great lesson:
You have to work hard to make it to the top.

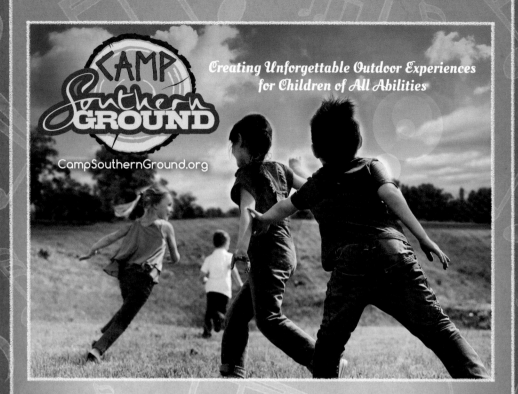

Creating Unforgettable Outdoor Experiences
for Children of All Abilities

CampSouthernGround.org

Room Makeovers for
Children with Long-Term Illness

sunshineonaranneyday.com